Once Upon A Dream

Unleashing Creativity

Edited By Briony Kearney

First published in Great Britain in 2024 by:

Young Writers

Young Writers
Remus House
Coltsfoot Drive
Peterborough
PE2 9BF
Telephone: 01733 890066
Website: www.youngwriters.co.uk

All Rights Reserved
Book Design by Ashley Janson
© Copyright Contributors 2024
Softback ISBN 978-1-83565-766-9
Printed and bound in the UK by BookPrintingUK
Website: www.bookprintinguk.com
YB0605AZ

FOREWORD

Welcome Reader, to a world of dreams.

For Young Writers' latest competition, we asked our writers to dig deep into their imagination and create a poem that paints a picture of what they dream of, whether it's a make-believe world full of wonder or their aspirations for the future.

The result is this collection of fantastic poetic verse that covers a whole host of different topics. Let your mind fly away with the fairies to explore the sweet joy of candy lands, join in with a game of fantasy football, or you may even catch a glimpse of a unicorn or another mythical creature. Beware though, because even dreamland has dark corners, so you may turn a page and walk into a nightmare!

Whereas the majority of our writers chose to stick to a free verse style, others gave themselves the challenge of other techniques such as acrostics and rhyming couplets. We also gave the writers the option to compose their ideas in a story, so watch out for those narrative pieces too!

Each piece in this collection shows the writers' dedication and imagination – we truly believe that seeing their work in print gives them a well-deserved boost of pride, and inspires them to keep writing, so we hope to see more of their work in the future!

CONTENTS

Allerton Bywater Primary School, Castleford

Freddie Hinks (9)	1
Lucy Evans (9)	2
Elsie Hirst (8)	3
Ava Worspop (9)	4
Olivia-Rose Crozier (8)	5

Eversley Primary School, Pitsea

Rhoda John (10)	6
Amilie Dunmore (10)	7
Isla Allen (10)	8
Samuel McCullim (10)	10

Gardners Lane Primary School, Cheltenham

Hannah Odumuyiwa (11)	11
Charis Arikawe (11)	12
Bryan Njoku (10)	13
Eliza Henson (7)	14
Summer Likeman (11)	15
Gabriella Ncube (11)	16
Amelia Lay (10)	17
Daisie Rosemary Ann (11)	18
Samanyu Rayaprolu (11)	19
Divit Sonune (8)	20
Lillith Lilly Evans (8)	21
Desislava Ivanova (9)	22
Yug Kataria (11)	23
Sanumi Ranaweera Arachchige (11)	24
Johann Adedipe (11)	25
Ashleigh Jones (11)	26
Brooke Martin (8)	27

Genesis Chikwena	28
Ronnie Opre (8)	29
Max Radford (11)	30

Highcliffe Primary School, Birstall

Ellie May (7)	31
Tiana Chauhan (8)	32
Harley-Temujin Ashton (8)	33
Shay Mistry (8)	34
Lilly Adams (8)	35
Anaya Patel (8)	36
Jainil Valand (8)	37
Dhruv Keshwala (7)	38
Kiyanna Lal (8)	39
Archie Roe (8)	40
Sophia Elson (8)	41
Jack Clark (8)	42
Raeya Chouhan (7)	43
Noah Melbourne (8)	44
Gurtej Kalsi (8)	45
Josh Brown	46
Nilay Mistry (8)	47
Anaya Shriya Patel (8)	48
Darcy Ince (8)	49
Seb Dingee (8)	50
Anaya Ava Kanani (8)	51

Hillside Avenue Primary And Nursery School, Norwich

Abigail Evans (9)	52
Arissa (9)	54
Ayan Abir (9)	55
Sienna Fairall (9)	56
Alex Crowhurst (9)	57

Zoe Asamoah (9) 58
Ava-Primrose Durrant (9) 59

Kents Hill Park School, Kents Hill

Erin Obinwa (11) 60
Leah Ashour (10) 61
Mercy Akinyemi (11) 62
Harraj Garewal (10) 63

Kippax Ash Tree Primary School, Kippax

Alice Emmett (10) 64
Niamh Wilkinson (10) 65
Emily Long (10) 66
Romeo Justo (10) 67
Pheobe Allison (10) 68
Stanislav Sukhov (10) 69
Jamie Brennan (10) 70
April Jessey (10) 71

Loders Primary Academy, Loders

Florence Bond (9) 72
Maisy Andrews (10) 74
Dominic White (9) 76
Khloe Shaw (11) 78
Hugo Battershell (8) 80
Sophia Chilcott-Moyes (8) 81
Grace Ellis (10) 82
Rosa Csano (10) 83
George Hughes (8) 84
Joseph Busk (10) 85
Wilber Hancock (8) 86
Freya Smith (10) 87
Seraphina Hancock (10) 88
Beatrice Ada Wheadon-Leaf (9) 89
Toby Smith (10) 90
Sofia Linnell (10) 91
Thomas Seprenyi-Batten (7) 92
Lizzie Petrie (10) 93
Paige Underwood (8) 94
Francis White (7) 95

Hermione Wheadon-Leaf (11) 96
Kiera McGuinness (8) 97
Albie Richardson-Todd (8) 98
Lily Seprenyi-Batten (7) 99
Martha Renshaw (8) 100
Mia Andrews (8) 101
Ella Wiscombe (9) 102
Elsie Shaw (8) 103
Michael Hughes (7) 104

Lote Tree Primary School, Foleshill

Manha Khan (10) 105
Suraiya Limbada (11) 106
Aaminah Rashid (11) 108
Abubakar Hussein (10) 109

Oldbury Park Primary School, Worcester

Sayon Irugalbandara (9) 110
Frederic Dollochin (9) 112
Caitlin Wheal (8) 113
Emily Eden (9) 114
Jacob Shaw (9) 116
Josie Stone (9) 117
Arlo Holding (8) 118
Addison Roper (9) 119
Archie Shellam (9) 120
Geordie Shellam (9) 121
Cassidy Konzvo (9) 122
Bobby Morris (8) 123
Beatrix Richardson (9) 124
Ivy Cartwright (9) 126
Timur Kircu (9) 127

Petworth Primary School, Petworth

Maggie Gambs (10) 128
Bethany Kent (10) 130
Sienna Boddy (9) 131
Lyla Anderson (10) 132

Springfield Academy, Darlington

Daisy-Mai Catherine (10)	133
Paige Hodgson (10)	134
Joshua Tang (10)	136
Theo Aldus (11)	137
Brian Lin (11)	138
Tyler Thompson (10)	140
Preeya Aujla (11)	141
Neave Coglan (11)	142
Jacob Bullock (10)	143
Romany-Rose Mcmain (11)	144
Jessica Wilson (11)	145
Charlie Hauxwell (11)	146

St Edmund's Catholic Primary School, Milwall

Lennie Clements (9)	147
Vanessa Plaka (7)	148
Milan Jambrich (8)	150
Penny Page (9)	152
Porus Sabharwal (7)	153
Nehvika Arora (7)	154
Aashvi Mohila (8)	155
Lily Jeon (9)	156
Talita Quintana Fortunato De Carvalho (8)	157
Gene Cutler (8)	158
Antonia Parsons	159
Esmé-Rose Murphy (8)	160
Hazel John-Lewis (8)	161
Zakaria Ahmed (9)	162
Lacey Clements (9)	163
Rithvik Jijin (9)	164

Tummery Primary School, Omagh

Lara Brogan (8)	165
Maddie Quinn (9)	166
Tierna O'Neill (8)	167
Nico Simpson (9)	168
Quinn McDermott (8)	169
Hannah McCormac (8)	170

Ellie Sheridan (8)	171
Dara O'Neill (8)	172
Rosie Barrett (9)	173
Karen Gibson (8)	174
Dara Doherty (8)	175
Luke Brogan (9)	176
Lauren Golden (8)	177
Christopher Mimnagh (8)	178

Whitegate End Primary & Nursery School, Oldham

Oscar Baines (9)	179
Lucas Yao (8)	180
Harry Beaumont (8)	181
Emily Shenton (9)	182
Billy Whaley (9)	183

Yeoford Community Primary School, Yeoford

Oliver Thomas (9)	184
Amelia Abbott (11)	185
Ellie Clarke (8)	186

THE CREATIVE WRITING

The Day Being A Football Player

First, he woke up and had a stretch. He got dressed and went downstairs for breakfast. He went outside and practised football so he was ready for the big important match in the afternoon at Elland Road. When he was practising, he felt very nervous to play the match, but he didn't want to let down the team on the day of the match. It was just a few hours until the big match against Man United in the Champions League.

When he got there, he was greeted by his players and then got greeted by some fans. He was in the changing room, getting ready for the match. It was just two minutes until the match and he was about to walk onto the pitch and see all the fans.

It was kick-off, he had the ball and got it into the net. The fans went crazy. The match ended 3-2, he won the important match that he had to win.

Freddie Hinks (9)
Allerton Bywater Primary School, Castleford

Dance The Night Away

D own go the lights
A ll ready for the night
N o turning back now
C urtains swish open
E veryone's here, my legs feel frozen

T *hud, thud*, goes my heart
H ear now, the show's about to start
E nergy fills the room

N othing prepared me for the big boom
I looked out into the large room
G lancing to my side
H ere I go to my stride
T utu twirling all around

A cro dancers on the ground
W histling and clapping from the crowd
A magical feeling, I'm so proud
Y es, it's over, I'm on top of the clouds.

Lucy Evans (9)
Allerton Bywater Primary School, Castleford

A Dream

Once upon a warm, summer night,
under the twinkling stars,
my mum tucked me into bed tight.
A short while later,
I fell into a deep dream.
I was with my friend
and we walked into an enchanted forest,
a twinkling forest,
it was beautiful.
As we were walking, we bumped into a cat,
and this cat had a hat
with a big black cap!
His name was Tap.
Tap showed me something wonderful -
a money tree
with a few honeybees,
they had lots of honey,
the honeybees had wobbly knees.
They had wobbly knees because
they tried to sneeze.
Me and my friend dropped to our knees,
crying tears of laughter.

Elsie Hirst (8)
Allerton Bywater Primary School, Castleford

Rain

Bombarded by droplets
Falling on my face
I reached into my pocket
And quickened my pace

Every step I stepped
Every breath I breathed
Every bird I heard
Reminded me of home

The warm fireplace
Crackling loudly in the corner
In a homely, happy haze
That little bit warmer

Then I am brought back to
The merciless iced, east winds
On this dreary day
Feeling blue
Listening to the creaking of the swings
And being blown away
Bombarded by the droplets
Falling on my face.

Ava Worspop (9)
Allerton Bywater Primary School, Castleford

Party Night

P utting on my dress, ready for fun
A lways late, so got to run
R eady for a laugh and a night to remember
T his is going to be the best night ever!
Y ou knock on my door, we're on our way

N ot looking back, to the par-tay!
I t's loud, it's shiny and everyone's here
G etting drinks and shouting, "Cheers!"
H aving a dance in the bright lights
T hat's what I love about these nights.

Olivia-Rose Crozier (8)
Allerton Bywater Primary School, Castleford

Whispers From The Rooftop

I roam the rooftop, a silhouette of night,
A black cat's secret, a world in different sight.
I roam the high peaks where the gashing winds howl,
And when the city lights and darkness slowly unfold.

My eyes gleam bright like the twinkling stars above,
Reflecting the moon with a gentle love.
I prowl and pace with whispers low,
The secrets kept here, only I know.

The world below, a distant hum,
A distant roar, a city's thrum.
I'm apart from it, yet a part,
A sentinel of darkness and heart.

Below my feet is where the secrets began,
Underneath me in this cosy home was a group of young me.
The secret stories that they told in whispers and sighs,
As I sat here, watching in the city skies.

But when the dawn breaks and night starts to depart,
I quickly vanish too, leaving only my heart.
For in the shadows, I've found my home,
Where the wind whispers secrets on the rooftop and I am alone.

Rhoda John (10)
Eversley Primary School, Pitsea

Once Upon A Dream

In my dream
I'm worshipped and loved
Like a queen on my throne
I am a living legend.

In my dream
Supporters look up to me
I guide my followers
People want to be me

In my dream
Me and twin make videos
We make people laugh
I'd be delighted to do this forever

In my dream
I get off my plane at NYC
Everybody knows me
I love my job!

Amilie Dunmore (10)
Eversley Primary School, Pitsea

My Dream

In my dream
unicorns can meow.
The sky is pink with glittery raindrops.
The trees and clouds are made out of cotton candy.
There are singing flowers and plants made of cupcakes.

In my dream
my friends come with me to Cotton Candy Land.
My cat comes too.
My cat also has wings
so he can fly up to the marshmallow moon.

In my dream
I am in Cotton Candy World.
Everything is sugar and sweet.
Cotton candy grass, cotton candy trees.
Everything you could imagine.
It seems like it's so real!

In my dream
I feel excited
I feel happy
and a bit confused.
Also wondering how can this dream be real?

In my dream
all of my friends eat all of the cotton candy,
even the clouds.
We eat all of the trees, all of the clouds,
even the plants made of cupcakes.

Isla Allen (10)
Eversley Primary School, Pitsea

Once Upon A Dream

In my dream
The sky is green
Dogs can fly and
Cats are stretchy

In my dream
I'm on my fire-breathing dragon
At the top of my castle

In my dream
Footballers can moonwalk
And pirate ships can fly

In my dream
Dinosaurs aren't extinct
And I'm very famous.

Samuel McCullim (10)
Eversley Primary School, Pitsea

Good Things Begin

Good things begin to happen
I have been uplifted and taken to higher places
Being successful, passing all my exams
And making everyone
Especially my hometown
Proud
Specifically my parents
Since then, it has been a new beginning
As I can remember
My parents were my mentor and my guardian
They were always proud of me
When I felt like giving up
As time went by
I knew in my mind
I wanted to make them proud
They were my joy and happiness
And living my childhood dream of graduating and
acquiring degrees to the the highest of choosing field
All thanks to those who believed in me
And made me who I am and what to be

Hannah Odumuyiwa (11)
Gardners Lane Primary School, Cheltenham

Dream Journey

D ay is bright, then comes the night
R unning to be on time, to bring dreams and delight
E veryone has either a dream or nightmares
A puzzling conspiracy, but something wrong
M ine is different, there are both dreams and nightmares

J oy can be found, so can fear, all in one…
O ver the darkness, on top, is the light
U rgh, I groan as I struggle and scream as loud as I can
R oaming around, finally, seeing the light
N ow I am free!
E verything so nice and nothing to complain about
Y awn, I open my eyes, oh, it was all a dream.

Charis Arikawe (11)
Gardners Lane Primary School, Cheltenham

My Hero Academia

M idoriya is the main character
Y oung, handsome, green-haired boy

H e wants to become strong
E ven though he is quirkless
R ound and round, his feelings go
O ver angry and over sad

A fter that, he found a quirk
C alled one for all
A ll might is stronger
D estroying villains left and right
E ven he is not that perfect
M astering all for one is hard
I zuku Midoriya became his dream, a strong hero
A master became of all might, teaching Midoriya.

Bryan Njoku (10)
Gardners Lane Primary School, Cheltenham

The Fat Spider And The Beautiful Ladybird

Once upon a time
A ladybird did climb
Up to the top of the tree
With a large swarm of bees
What did she see?
But a big fat spider, drinking a cup of tea
The spider bellowed in a very deep voice,
"Who goes there? You must make a choice!"
The ladybird shivered and said quietly,
"What do you want from me?"
The big fat spider smiled happily and said,
"Will you go make me a fresh cup of tea?"
The spider and the ladybird sat in the tree
While drinking their cups of tea.

Eliza Henson (7)
Gardners Lane Primary School, Cheltenham

A Moth's Dream

My dream is simple for a small moth
To see, up front, a lamp without a cover cloth

It's hard to sweep out and in from gaps
Of the windows, doors and cracks

It's not easy for a tiny thing
Just make sure the exterminator's door doesn't ring

Looking back, not paying attention to the front
Wham!

I hit a bald bulb, no cover, no cloth
A dream has been fulfilled
But one thing, to be surrounded by light
Once again.

Summer Likeman (11)
Gardners Lane Primary School, Cheltenham

My Dreamland

It's upside-down in Dreamland
The sun is as shining as a diamond
The sky is covered in clouds

Perfect little man
On the first of May
The sun appeared so bright

The man was so little
He was humble, perfect and lovely
Enemies were coming for the little man

He was lonely
And his wife died fifteen years ago
The little man didn't know what to do
Because everybody in the area didn't like him.

Gabriella Ncube (11)
Gardners Lane Primary School, Cheltenham

My Dream Covered In Snow

I wake up in the night
awakened by the light
glowing, shining so bright.
There, a figure that stands alone
painting my home with her
white fuzzy blanket
and the window panes
covered in frost, ice bunting.
She twirls up my street
afraid of awakening the people asleep
enchanting me with a frosty glow
she leaps and twirls but wait, oh!
She's gone, vanished, oh, but wait
all that's left is a frosty old cape.

Amelia Lay (10)
Gardners Lane Primary School, Cheltenham

The Passion About Horse Riding

My dream, in the future, I am a horse rider
I have always wanted to be a horse rider
I have seen myself on a white horse
That evening, the sunset was beaming
The horse was a beautiful white horse
I have never been able to ride a horse
But in the dream, I could
It was confusing
Everything was upside-down
I was upside-down
It didn't feel like real life
Always remember, follow your dreams
And be passionate about it.

Daisie Rosemary Ann (11)
Gardners Lane Primary School, Cheltenham

My Dream

M y dream is a world where
Y ou can be anything, there are

D ragons, castles, knights and
R obots and red rivers
E verywhere, chocolates, sweets and ice cream
A nd everything you want
M y dream is paradise

W orry and pain never present
O verly affectionate
R espect is neverending
L ove and affection, where
D reams come true.

Samanyu Rayaprolu (11)
Gardners Lane Primary School, Cheltenham

Chasing Dragons

In the night, in my dream,
I chase the dragons,
In my beautiful wagon.
I want to make them my pet,
Because they fly like a jet.
They are as strong as a rock,
I want them to talk.
I want them to protect my castle,
I want the dragons to cuddle.
My dragons throw fireballs,
And protect my castle walls.
Suddenly, my eyes are wide open,
And I see no one.
I really hope to see a real one.

Divit Sonune (8)
Gardners Lane Primary School, Cheltenham

The Lightning Fire

We went on an adventure
And we saw a mountain
Covered in flowers
We went up the mountain
Went with my family
We saw a cave
We went inside
And saw a cover over a picture
We brought it out and looked at it
It was a famous picture
We gave it to the museum
We got a lot of money
For finding a famous picture
We saw a little girl trapped in ice
We saved her
I was happy!

Lillith Lilly Evans (8)
Gardners Lane Primary School, Cheltenham

Dreams Are Wonderful

Every single dream makes people smile!
Every single dream makes everyone go towards success!
Every single dream brings people together to do a goal!
That's why everyone should dream, make their dreams come true,
And they will bring them success!
That's why dreams are wonderful!
Dream, smile, do good and the world will become
A better place for us little children
With wonderful dreaming!

Desislava Ivanova (9)
Gardners Lane Primary School, Cheltenham

The Day I Met XXX

In the middle of the night, I woke up in a dream. I was in some sort of heaven. I looked around. I saw a guy with dreads, half black, half blue.
I moved closer, I was two metres in distance from him. I looked at him. He looked familiar. I asked, "What is your name?"
"X... X... Xtentation!" he murmured.
I freaked out. He was my favourite rapper that sadly died. And suddenly, my mum woke me up.

Yug Kataria (11)
Gardners Lane Primary School, Cheltenham

The Freezing Dream

It was a dream
In a freezing field
It was pitch-black
Glow of stars
In the free breeze

Something was screaming
From the frozen lake
I went closer to have a good look
Oh no, it was a dying polar bear
It didn't seem harmful at all
It was moaning as it needed help

My mum woke me up
Before it was done
It was the best dream
That I ever had.

Sanumi Ranaweera Arachchige (11)
Gardners Lane Primary School, Cheltenham

Dreamland

D reamland, the dark and mysterious world
R ed sky everywhere
E merald ice cream in the air
A nime people everywhere
M angoes jumping and waiting to be eaten
L ego people dancing in the moonlight
A mazing games to play all day
N obody to stop you from playing
D reamland is the best place to be.

Johann Adedipe (11)
Gardners Lane Primary School, Cheltenham

Potions

P erfect little room
O f potions that meet the eye
T he sparkling large flames dancing around the class
I magining all the effects of the sizzling potions
O ld tired books scattered randomly
N otebooks left behind from lessons
S moke opens into the room, there's nothing there to stop you from anything.

Ashleigh Jones (11)
Gardners Lane Primary School, Cheltenham

Dream

Your imagination is your creation of dreams
It feels like real life, but not what it seems
The feeling is real, but sometimes it's not
The dreams might be cold or very hot
If it's not a dream, it's a nightmare
It might be magical, but it could be a scare
So let's all go together and hold tight onto our bedtime bear.

Brooke Martin (8)
Gardners Lane Primary School, Cheltenham

The Little Unicorn Shooting Star

In my dreams, every night
Space horses fly with colours bright
Starlit and moonbeam manes
One by one, they pass me by in the rainbow
And I always see shooting stars
One day, I saw a little star
It was a cute star
And I saw a unicorn
It was colourful and magical.

Genesis Chikwena
Gardners Lane Primary School, Cheltenham

Whispers To The Night Sky

I whispered to the stars about you
How your smile shimmers like morning dew
How your laughter is so entertaining
You're like stars now
Beautiful and peaceful at night
That is what I whispered to the stars about you.

Ronnie Opre (8)
Gardners Lane Primary School, Cheltenham

Dreams

In the future, I want to be a YouTuber
and be successful in gaming
and get lots of views
and I would do some crazy challenges,
like one chest challenge
as well as rainbow skin.

Max Radford (11)
Gardners Lane Primary School, Cheltenham

Unicorns

In the night, when you imagine a unicorn pops up in your dream, you will realise something bright is under your bed. You check under your bed and you see a flash. You don't know what it is. Your mum checks on you, but you say you saw something flash under your bed. Your mum will just say you are dreaming, not seeing. When you are dreaming and seeing. Then your mum leaves your room, then you go to sleep. Then you wake up and it was a unicorn. It picks you up and you're in the sky. You go into the clouds and there, you're at the Kingdom of Clouds. Then the unicorn brings you back home and then you're fast asleep. Then it's morning, you tell your mum the adventure.

Ellie May (7)
Highcliffe Primary School, Birstall

Enchanted Forest

Once, I was walking with my dog
When there became a lot of fog
I couldn't see where I was going
And I walked into a forest without knowing
The fog soon cleared and I could see
A magnificent forest in front of me!
There were fairies flying everywhere
There were talking mushrooms here and there
I saw some unicorns ahead
I walked up to them and I said,
"Do you live here?" they replied,
"Yes, we do, come inside."
They led me into their home
It really was quite comfortable
So we had some food, mushrooms to eat
And it was dark, so we all went to sleep.

Tiana Chauhan (8)
Highcliffe Primary School, Birstall

A Dream

A shiny, shimmering castle,
A rainbow wolf as cute and soft as a teddy,
But wants to eat you sometimes,
A flying car with shimmering blue circles,
Underneath the car with a shiny silver paint coat,
Do you know what it is?
It's a DeLorean!
But now it's bloody red,
It's got wings, a tail with spikes on it,
It's colossal, it's a dragon!
I saw the cool, smart GOAT,
Called Cristiano Ronaldo,
Dinosaurs and more,
I was in a black, purple, pinky, yellow sky,
With me, was a red-orange-furred creature,
A sharp black nose, teeth like a katana.

Harley-Temujin Ashton (8)
Highcliffe Primary School, Birstall

Football

F antastic football players surrounded the football pitch
O verjoyed, the football players started to kick the ball
O h no, the ball said, "Dance like you're twerking."
T errible football players said, "Just score!"
B um-bum, I twerked at who is reading
A ll of the football players tried to kick the ball
L ook, said the footballers, "Footballs are singing."
L ick the ground to save us. "Blech, what?"

Shay Mistry (8)
Highcliffe Primary School, Birstall

Gymnastics

G lowing bars and beams
Y our gymnastics team
M ay practice until they say
N ow I'm ready, no more practising for today
A t the competition tomorrow morning
S orry to say, I may be yawning
T alking to my friends all day
I n the gym, when someone comes, I say, no way!
C artwheels on beams, flips on bars
S ide-flipping past gymnastic stars.

Lilly Adams (8)
Highcliffe Primary School, Birstall

Once Upon A Dream

Once upon a time, I was in the sky. I was walking on white pom-pom clouds. It was a dream to be in the clouds. Then I found a portal, so I went in. It took me to a pegasus. It was rainbow and its horn was shiny and gold as a golden bar and glittery. She was as white as a cloud. She had bright glittery hair. So I went on her saddle and rode it in the sky. But something happened, I had to go.

Anaya Patel (8)
Highcliffe Primary School, Birstall

The Nightmare!

As you close your eyes at nighttime.
Scary stuff appears, like skeletons and ghosts!!
But only comes when you are asleep...
If you wake up in the middle of the night
and the scary stuff is there still
It can go away like the dust!
When you wake up, you will feel a bit weird because the scary stuff has been in your room.

Jainil Valand (8)
Highcliffe Primary School, Birstall

The Gigantic Dream

One day, I was on red-hot Mars, fighting a pack of aliens. Red versus blue, who was gonna lose? Fighting on a red planet, extremely hot and hard to beat. I slammed some bears and got a jar and slammed a guy on the bright moon. I hit him in a jar, flying on the moon. To be done, reds won. And I said, "See you soon."

Dhruv Keshwala (7)
Highcliffe Primary School, Birstall

Gymnastics

G lowing bars and beams
Y ikes, squawk
M arch until I drop
N appies as babies cry
A pples fall on my head
S omersaults as I hit the ground
T ill I came off the beam
I vy lights
C artwheels
S ights are not clear.

Kiyanna Lal (8)
Highcliffe Primary School, Birstall

Football

F ootball rolls up to the player
O ut the white lines
O range ball comes back to play again
T ackle the player
B ouncing ball rolled to a player
A gain, again, again and again
L ike a rugby ball
L ike a fantastic rugby ball.

Archie Roe (8)
Highcliffe Primary School, Birstall

Excellent Dancing

D azzling spotlight in the air
A round and around, the dancers go
N othing can stop me going on stage
C reative people dancing
I nspiring dancers telling me to
N ightmares that night, stick in my head
G lowing in my eyes.

Sophia Elson (8)
Highcliffe Primary School, Birstall

Famous

F ascinating castle, just not yet
A small cottage, very cheap
M aybe it might get bigger
O h so fascinating, it did get bigger
U h, and I own a chocolate factory of chocolate
S uch a nice castle made of rainbows.

Jack Clark (8)
Highcliffe Primary School, Birstall

Fantasy

F lying creatures all around
A mazing fluffy clouds like candyfloss
N ever going to leave
T ime to meet the pegasus
A mazing dreams
S parkly wings
Y ummy milkshakes for all.

Raeya Chouhan (7)
Highcliffe Primary School, Birstall

Ronaldo

R onaldo is the GOAT
O h yeah, goal!
N o, so close
A udience cheering happily
L oud cheers in the stadium
D o it, Ronaldo!
O h, so close.

Noah Melbourne (8)
Highcliffe Primary School, Birstall

Football

I saw a football
I saw the big moon
I saw the football player
I saw the trash bin
I heard the football hit the wall
I want a ball
I saw the big light
Look, that is nice.

Gurtej Kalsi (8)
Highcliffe Primary School, Birstall

The Stay Down

Thought as like a stadium
The lights went on and off
The lights went on and off
It went on for hours
Bouncy ball
Annoying football
Laughing players
Laughing players.

Josh Brown
Highcliffe Primary School, Birstall

Future

F antastic flying cars
U nique dogs
T reats that have dog poop in them
U nique silly bins
R ed sparkling skyscrapers
E pic cool robots.

Nilay Mistry (8)
Highcliffe Primary School, Birstall

Dream

D ay and night, you have dreams
R are dreams happen every day
E very day, dream every day, exciting dreams
A mazing dreams
M agic like a wand.

Anaya Shriya Patel (8)
Highcliffe Primary School, Birstall

Everlasting Dance

D ancing around the world
A mazing tumbling on the floor
N ever gonna stop
C an dance all my life
E verlasting dancing around the world.

Darcy Ince (8)
Highcliffe Primary School, Birstall

Once Upon A Dream

D inosaur dream
R ound castle
E ek! A flying creature
A mazing features all around
M ythical creatures hunting me down.

Seb Dingee (8)
Highcliffe Primary School, Birstall

Beautiful Dreams

D ance in the dark, sparkling sky
R ainbow dresses
E verlasting dreams
A mazing dreams
M arble diamonds.

Anaya Ava Kanani (8)
Highcliffe Primary School, Birstall

The Spartan Myth

A lexious was mainly called the Eagle-Beaver, he's brave, mercenary, powerful

S trange things in Athens, Perikles was killed by... the hero of the cult, Kassandra

T he waves bow to her in fear, the great battle was coming up, Athens or Sparta?

R apidly, the seas are calm for Athens but not Sparta, they terrorise the ships

A thens can't live a day longer, we need to fight or die

N ow the battle has come, on the island of Pylos were the enemies, Alexious and Kassandra

G radually, Athens won, but Sparta would be back...

E ruptingly, Alexious gathered them together, "We will fight again."

O n the sand was Mater, Alexious promised her that Kassandra would return

D isturbing news, Alexious is planning to attack. "Kill him."

Y awning Alexious would kill Kassandra with the best sword and armour

S urprisingly, he killed her, but only the stunt double

S tunt double, what do you mean? She's after me, give me her location!
E xcitingly, the cult was gone, so was Athens, Sparta had victory again!
Y ay! We did it! Pater would be so proud.

Abigail Evans (9)
Hillside Avenue Primary And Nursery School, Norwich

The Enchanting Flower

Legend talks of the enchanting flower
If you touch it, you uncover its magical power
It will always make your wishes come true
If you're curious about mysteries, it'll reveal clues
If you ever feel down
It will treat you with respect, and that you're royalty with a crown
The enchanting flower is a valuable item
If some crooks want war, it won't fight them
There shall always be peace in its petals
And it can break any metal
Although when it gets angry, it's hot as a kettle
But if I could just touch it, I would give it a medal
So we always have to keep sacred and special
We never ever say a word
Because we don't want to be overheard
And hopefully, people think it was a mystery
And it will be passed down in history
Until a curious child sees it
And says, "I'm going to write a poem, it's an interesting sight to see
Just like me!"

Arissa (9)
Hillside Avenue Primary And Nursery School, Norwich

Mother Nature

Every night, I dream
A world of nature that is green
Mother Nature's love is as powerful as a silent mountain
a fierce storm, a graceful rain
As divine as a calm ocean
Nature has imagination,
it is the world of creation
Nature, you cannot capture
But you can follow the path of adventure
This place, you are not to torture
But to love and nurture
Nature is not cruel, it is not glam
Nature is full of liveliness, it is full of love
In this wild starry night
I have a dream so beautiful and bright.

Ayan Abir (9)
Hillside Avenue Primary And Nursery School, Norwich

Talking Shed

T errifying croaky voice coming from our shed
A bit of me wants to hide under the bed
L urking shadows come from the window
K nowing my brain, it's going to blow
I 'm a monster, I will eat you up!
N ow I am going out with protection that is a drinking cup
G oing out of the door

S omething is still moving and I saw
H e came to me and it was Dad!
E verything I thought was wrong, I was very mad
D addy, come home now, into a nice warm bed.

Sienna Fairall (9)
Hillside Avenue Primary And Nursery School, Norwich

Feelings

Feelings can hurt, feelings can make you happy
Feelings can do everything
Your feelings show to other people
So you know how you feel
Feelings can make you feel famous
Feelings can make you run away from home
Or something else
Feelings can make you become a footballer
A teacher, maybe even a dancer
Feelings help us
If we didn't have feelings
We wouldn't cry
We wouldn't be happy
We wouldn't be angry.

Alex Crowhurst (9)
Hillside Avenue Primary And Nursery School, Norwich

Mina's Marvellous Mysterious Museum

"Welcome to Mina's Marvellous Mysterious Museum!
With music spreading far and wide from city to city,
From skylines to headlines,
And from bedrooms to school rooms.
Drop off your unwanted items and stay,
While we make them a masterpiece on display!
Like no other place in the UK,
Or other environments of the world,
Welcome, everybody, to Mina's Marvellous Mysterious Museum!"

Zoe Asamoah (9)
Hillside Avenue Primary And Nursery School, Norwich

The Calm Clouds

The clouds drift, the clouds sway,
They are there every day,
Swirling shapes of candyfloss,
The only white in the beautiful, endless sky,
Although you forget they are there,
I can definitely confirm they are very, very enchanting,
So you must pay to look up,
As nothing is as elegant as them.

Ava-Primrose Durrant (9)
Hillside Avenue Primary And Nursery School, Norwich

A Dream Of Sunlight And Darkness

Twisted trees loom over the murky river
The vines brush against me, making me shiver
I hear the shrill shrieks of the creatures of the night
While the thick fog blurs my sight

Green trees sway above the crystal-clear stream
The flowery vines twist together like a dress' seam
The birds compose a sweet melody
The beautiful sunrays make me feel fluttery

An ongoing battle disturbs the peace
Sunlight blankets the darkness in a warm fleece
Darkness tries to fight back, but its attempt fails
The sunlight rises as darkness pales

Sunlight whisks me away to a faraway land
Where tall hills and steep mountains stand
Stallions of whites, greys and blacks
Gallop closer and offer their backs

Everything fades into the distance
Everything, including my real existence...

Erin Obinwa (11)
Kents Hill Park School, Kents Hill

The Wood Of Good And Evil

Once upon a dream,
In the middle of the night,
I sneak out of bed to the Wood of Good and Evil,
Where my dreams take flight.
Some unicorns on the cotton candy floor,
Want nothing more than to gallop some more.
One by one, they pass by
in the magical, sparkling sky.
However, on the other side of this enchanting place,
It has a totally different face.
Angry clowns juggling with fire,
Only liked by a ghastly vampire.
Blood-curdling dragons soar through the air,
The most unwelcoming ingredient to your nightmare.
But now the sun is rising,
Dawn has arrived,
My alarm clock rings,
I feel my teddy on my shoulder,
Gladly relieved it is finally over.

Leah Ashour (10)
Kents Hill Park School, Kents Hill

Once Upon A Dream

Once upon a dream,
every night when you go to sleep.
Once upon a dream,
all the magic starts to form as quiet as it can be.
Once upon a dream,
when ogres and giants ruled the sky.
Once upon a dream,
that's when the light starts to die.
'Cause they stomp with a shout
and they jump with a pout and they scream until you wake...
And realise it was all...
once upon a dream!

Mercy Akinyemi (11)
Kents Hill Park School, Kents Hill

Exploring A Nightmare

Nowhere like this place
Has ever been such a disgrace.

It's filled up by a great big spider
And you can only eat stuff that's bitter.

No video games
Just school and work all day.

Suddenly, an eerie scream pops in your ear
And you wake up
All crumpled in bed.

Now I'm free
At least 'til next sleep.

Harraj Garewal (10)
Kents Hill Park School, Kents Hill

The Shining Nightmare

Nightmare, nightmare, dream so bright,
Let your sparkle come to life,
If your sparkle isn't bright,
Let's get up to all the hype,
If your hype isn't so high,
Let's get out in the light,
If you think it's too bright,
Let's travel in the night.
Find a spot in the park,
And stargaze into the night,
The night's so dark,
And the stars are so bright,
I can't help but look all night.
I wait all day to see the stars,
Hoping, one day, I'd see a shooting star,
I've come so far to make my heart,
I wish I could just see a shooting star.
In my dreams, I am a superhero,
Flying through the night sky,
In the moonlight,
Suddenly, I wake up,
And talk about what I've been dreaming of
Through the night.

Alice Emmett (10)
Kippax Ash Tree Primary School, Kippax

The Creatures Of Ferret Forest

Once upon a dream,
It was just Emily and me,
We were lost in a forest,
Scared and scarred,
Like we were holding sacks of fear,
We heard something come near,
It looked half-spider,
Then it came like a glider,
Me and Emily stood still,
As we gently walked up the hill,
Suddenly, something flew by,
As I looked up in the midnight sky,
I saw a dragon waving goodbye,
I was very confused until...
I was back at home, huddled in my bed!

Niamh Wilkinson (10)
Kippax Ash Tree Primary School, Kippax

The Baby Dragon's Dreamland Flight

In a dream, one special night,
A baby dragon, small and bright,
With wings of blue and eyes of gold,
Appeared and stories soon were told,

We flew above the fields so green,
And saw sights no one had ever seen,
A unicorn with a shiny horn,
And friendly fairies newly born,

The baby dragon flew away,
Through the night and into day,
Morning came and he left my side,
But in my heart, he stays so bright.

Emily Long (10)
Kippax Ash Tree Primary School, Kippax

Summer

In the summer, I like to play
in the garden, all night and day.
I like to play baseball and basketball,
football is the best of all.
Ice cream is the dream,
but not sunscreen.
When it's summer, I play happily
with family.
Think of your dream summer,
I hope it is not a bummer.
The pool is cool,
and I'm looking forward to no school!
Woo! It is so hot,
give me a pot
of water over my head.

Romeo Justo (10)
Kippax Ash Tree Primary School, Kippax

Dreams Come True

Do you believe dreams come true?
Well I do! A little girl lies down in her bed,
waiting to get whisked away again and again.
But tonight's dream is a special one -
she gets whisked away
where dreams are made by little fairies all day.
She meets two fairies, one dreamy, one nightmare,
one good, one bad,
and an old little wizard called Snow Night.
Then she wakes up all happy and nice
and gets on with her day.

Pheobe Allison (10)
Kippax Ash Tree Primary School, Kippax

The Bald Man

As I walk and wait,
the bald man contemplates.
Some mountains are passing by,
some dragons are flying awry.
The man offers me some food,
and I do not refuse.
I am enjoying this meal,
good, it is, I feel.
Astronauts and dragons, I see,
weird, I agree.
As the day starts to faint,
the night sky starts to paint...

Stanislav Sukhov (10)
Kippax Ash Tree Primary School, Kippax

Fairy Land

Last night, I had a dream,
There was a beautiful stream,
Not a care in the world,
Fairies whirled and water swirled,
Last night, I had a dream,

Last night, I had a dream,
I followed a beautiful stream
To the magical Fairy Land,
Where there was beautiful white sand,
Last night, I had a dream.

Jamie Brennan (10)
Kippax Ash Tree Primary School, Kippax

Sweets

S omething happened! It was so
W eird, I found something, so I wanted to
E at it (just me being me) and once I did
E verything changed! I
T eleported to the new world, full of
S weets! I thought I was dreaming, it turns out I was.

April Jessey (10)
Kippax Ash Tree Primary School, Kippax

Meatball Lady

A tiny bowl of Cheetos clasped in my hand,
My hair done up in a rubber band,

The meatball mountains look tasty, with cheesy snow,
I look at the clock - it's time to go!

I climb to their secret entrance, I hop in,
Even though I'm in a rush, I could go for a spin!

Suddenly, a roar shakes my head,
It's even louder than my sister! I look ahead,

Oh no! It's as white as a blister!
I skid to the side of the sausage road then

The Ghostbusters shoot out,
They use their shrink-rays and aim!

The guns shoot mega-aggressive clowns out
To the monster, such a pain!

Then, a clown jumps onto me,
And with a whoosh of his magic wand,

He turns me into an Oreo!
"Sorry!" the clown says sarcastically,

"Oh, I meant, s-Oreos!"

Florence Bond (9)
Loders Primary Academy, Loders

The Forest Fright

I drifted off to sleep,
I heard a beep, beep, beep,
Leaping into my rainbow, chocolate, fudge drop house,
I met a wizard with a lemon drop mouse,
Who had to train it not to pounce,
Once I saw that horrible mouse,
I bounced and begged and thumped my way out,
That horrible mouse had a gigantic snout.

I was in a forest with lots of bright lights,
That I see every night,
I saw a red kite,
That gave me a fright,
I had a blurry sight,
That gave me a big bite,

Waiting for Christmas to come,
I have lots of rings,
I hope I get all my favourite things,
I saw Santa,
While my horse was doing a canter,
I had some Fanta
With the jolly fat man, Santa.

Somebody opened the door,
I knew I was very poor,
My feet were very sore,
Help me get off the floor.

Maisy Andrews (10)
Loders Primary Academy, Loders

There's A Monster In My Bedroom

There's a monster in my bedroom,
It tries to squeeze in,
Down goes the doorframe,
The monster's not thin.

There's a monster in my bedroom,
It tips up my drawers,
It thinks it's fun,
Nothing comes out, since my washing's not done.

There's a monster in my bedroom,
It jumps on my bed,
I'm still in it,
So it squashes my head.

There's a monster in my bedroom,
It finds all my stuff,
It tries some on,
But nothing's big enough.

There's a monster in my bedroom,
It's reading my books,

He does not seem to like them,
As he gives them strange looks.

There are now many chores
That I will not do,
There's a monster in my bedroom,
And you don't want one too.

Dominic White (9)
Loders Primary Academy, Loders

A Weird And Revolting Tale Of Villains

In the forest, far and wide
With my best buds on my side
My friend, Ella, with an umbrella
And the Grinch that will pinch

The trees moan and groan
Like old men that don't want to be thrown
Then, gloomy shadows came upon my path
Enforcing my great, mighty staff

It was Voldemort the great
With a bucket of paint
We had something hairy
It was a big fat fairy
She said, "Ouch!"
With a big fat pouch

Then she died of starvation
But she had a revelation!
Now it had a reason
For its treason

She had a big ray
That she played with all day
Now she went to prison
Because she had a vision

And in that vision was Khloe, me
Shining bright like a bee.

Khloe Shaw (11)
Loders Primary Academy, Loders

Haunted House

The haunted house has a mouse,
The mouse stays with a woodlouse,
People host parties with the ghosts,
But it wasn't a very good host,
Everyone shouts, "No ghosts! No ghosts!"
But that was part of the host.

I had a look at the haunted house,
With my mouse,
There was an old host,
I saw whipped cream, but I screamed,
There were ghosts at the old host,
The ghosts were cooking a roast,
But I already had some toast.

My mouse also screamed,
It started to run, but the ghosts found it fun,
The ghosts surrounded me all around,
I ran around them but I went through them,
Now I was having fun and the ghosts started to run,
I never went back to the haunted house.

Hugo Battershell (8)
Loders Primary Academy, Loders

Untitled

I put on my candyfloss dress,
I went outside to Ice Cream Marshmallow Land,
To have a picnic where the toffee cakes were missing from the basket,
Someone had stolen the toffee cake,
"Has someone stolen the toffee cake?" I asked,
The candyfloss deer said no,
I asked every animal to take it back,
So I went saying, "Oh giant ice cream scoop,"
Then I saw marshmallow bees,
I went to the queen bee who had the toffee cake,
I went to get my cake back,
The queen bee said, "I'm sorry, was that your cake?"
I said, "Yes, would you like to have a picnic with me?"
"Yes," said the queen bee,
Then I woke up in my room.

Sophia Chilcott-Moyes (8)
Loders Primary Academy, Loders

My Sweet Dream

I've drifted off into a dream of
Sugarplums and clotted cream
Where sugar petals form a stream
They dance and gleam just like whipped
Cream, but it is not what it would seem.
Below the gushing, luscious stream
There is a twist, now you will see
A marshmallow monster much
Bigger than me!
But I was brave, I stood strong and
Tall and said, "I'm not scared
I refuse to bawl!"
But then, something surprised me
Something so strange.
The marshmallow man said,
"Would you like some cake?"
I could hardly say no
But now, this is the end
So, I say my farewell
Goodbye, my dear friend.

Grace Ellis (10)
Loders Primary Academy, Loders

The Giraffe In A Balloon

I was walking through a jungle with vines and monkeys with a cold,
It seemed quite crazy, but it would never get old,
Then something caught my eye, it was a very weird sight,
A giant red balloon, which gave me a fright,
I walked a bit closer, my heart was beating fast,
I knew this moment would scare me, my heart will need a cast,
Then, all of a sudden, I heard giggles and laughs,
I looked through the balloon and there was a giraffe,
A monkey sneezed, which popped the balloon,
The giraffe got startled and made a funny tune,
The giraffe was glad and ran away,
And that was the end of my dream today.

Rosa Csano (10)
Loders Primary Academy, Loders

My Burger Came Alive!

I drifted to a far land, away from home,
When I saw the ground zoom,
I thought I saw my tomb,
Now, I saw me on the shoulders of Cliff,
A strong guy carrying me,
Then I saw something,
I saw a spider burger,
In the corner of my eye,
I saw Toby the flying beaver,
He hit the spider,
But he got hit by the impact and fell,
As soon as Toby fell,
The spider broke free,
As we ran as fast as we could,
We got hit and were about to be eaten,
I returned to the real world,
So I dreamt of something else,
The summer holidays.

George Hughes (8)
Loders Primary Academy, Loders

It's Upside-Down In Dreamland

It's upside-down in Dreamland,
the sky is blue and green.
I'm confused because I keep on moving,
I'm in the clouds, they are so mean.
I'm falling, I'm falling in the trees,
the marshmallow man gave me a cake,
he tricked me as I began to quake.
Then, suddenly, there was a monster,
he made me shake and shiver,
I looked at him so many times,
he jumped into the river.
And then he flipped the bed,
and I remembered the washing must go out!
I don't know what will happen next,
I might wake up and shout!

Joseph Busk (10)
Loders Primary Academy, Loders

Flying Beavers

Zoom! went the flying beaver, right past my long nose,
He shouted, "Help me! Get loads of Oreos!"
I ran, ran, ran, but it was no good,
As I couldn't catch them because of my hood.

I dodged giant monsters that ate my foot,
For some reason, they said, "Put candy on Moot!"
"Yes," I said as Moot is a giant foot
That spits fire much bigger than a tree.

Suddenly, a pea sat on me,
I realised it was time for me!
But I had to go,
So I said goodbye, my blue buffalo.

Wilber Hancock (8)
Loders Primary Academy, Loders

Once, In Your Dream

Pink fog fills the sky,
I'm too high in the sky,
The fog starts to shake and pop!
A house comes out,
I go in, slam! The door closes,
A cold breeze comes in,
Red eyes fill the room,
The sounds of whispering,
Saying, "Run, now! While you can!"
I try to get out,
I hear a bang!
And something says, "Wheee!"
And plop!
A fluffy, pink, candyfloss-coloured unicorn
Is sat at my feet.
The unicorn unlocks the door
And we are free,
And Elmo and Kermit were at the door.

Freya Smith (10)
Loders Primary Academy, Loders

The Game

I drifted off into a dream,
With radioactive frogs on my team,
We're in a stadium, ready to play,
We're against the gigantic dogs today,
We win the game,
But then the warthogs came,
They shot blue logs,
And hit six mogs,
Then pounded on the door,
'Cause they knew they'd broken the law,
The police come,
And they scream for their mum,
But she only beats their bottoms,
Shouting, "Not'em, Nottom!"

Seraphina Hancock (10)
Loders Primary Academy, Loders

My Teatime Dream

As I drifted off to sleep,
I opened my eyes to peep,
And saw a sign to say,
You've made it to Teatime Land today.

I looked around to see
A giant meatball in front of me,
I realised it was time for tea,
But I was stuck in a pile of spaghetti.

My friends, Florie and Wilber, helped me out,
To celebrate, we all ran about,
We laughed and laughed until we popped,
And that's where my dream stopped.

Beatrice Ada Wheadon-Leaf (9)
Loders Primary Academy, Loders

Land Of Dreams

I drifted off in the Land of Dreams
There was a ginormous parrot with large pointy teeth
Like a vampire, hunting and watching
For something good to eat
I felt like someone was following me
Frightened and on my own, I ran
Through the deep, dark, creepy forest
Chasing me was a huge orangutan!
Boom, wallop, crash, bash, bang
I looked around to see
This hairy, purple gorilla
Playing drums for me.

Toby Smith (10)
Loders Primary Academy, Loders

A Dream

I drifted into a dream,
a restaurant was right in front of me.
I could smell the delicious meatballs
calling my name over again,
whispering, "Sofia, Sofia, come on!"
I couldn't resist.
From down the corridor,
I could hear moans
from an unhappy cake,
"Why have you not eaten me yet?"
With determination on my face,
I picked up my fork
and picked up the past.

Sofia Linnell (10)
Loders Primary Academy, Loders

The Race

I'm on the racetrack, ready to race
With a cool rubber band, I forgot to tie my shoelace.
I'm ready to go, Sonic is too,
The race started, we go in a hurry to see who wins.
But Sonic runs as fast as he can,
He hits his leg on a peg,
A flying guinea pig pops out of nowhere, helping Sonic,
I'm in the lead, Sonic is behind me,
We both win, it's a tie.

Thomas Seprenyi-Batten (7)
Loders Primary Academy, Loders

The Weird African Dream

Blue, upside-down trees billow in the wind
Across the river, rainbow lizards skimmed
While flying giraffes filled the sky
Underground ducks ate apple pie
Then the alarm rang and my African dream dimmed.

Lizzie Petrie (10)
Loders Primary Academy, Loders

A Place Full Of Sweets

I drifted off to a place full of sweets,
I saw loads of candyfloss clouds,
There were lots of places to go and eat.
I was excited and confused
Because I didn't know where I was,
And I was lonely.
I saw a big friendly marshmallow man,
And he helped me find my way back home,
The marshmallow man went back to his family.

Paige Underwood (8)
Loders Primary Academy, Loders

Kung-Fu Panda

Bang! I hit my opponent off his feet and said he was dead meat,
I ran back to the temple and found out it was a pimple.

My master said I was faster than a plaster,
Then he went off to training, but I was flaming.

I went through the village and found a sausage in the garbage.

Francis White (7)
Loders Primary Academy, Loders

Nirvana

N o! Why am I here?
I t's Kurt Cobain with only one ear
R ight, I think it's time to run away
V ery quickly, I try to move my legs
A nnoyingly, they are trapped in-between some pegs!
N ow he's chasing me
A nd darkness is all I see.

Hermione Wheadon-Leaf (11)
Loders Primary Academy, Loders

Stripy Super Socks

I fell into a dream
There were super stripy socks
All around, being mean in my bedroom

The super stripy socks
Wouldn't get in their pairs
But the perfect polka dots
Do it on the stairs

The socks went outside at midnight
And caused mischief.

Kiera McGuinness (8)
Loders Primary Academy, Loders

Sonic 2

I'm in Sonic Land
When he was a baby
So was Tails
But he was in the pool, with the ball

I can see something blue and yellow
Oh, look, it's Sonic and Tails
I will look for Knuckles
It took weeks and weeks
Finally, I found him with Eggman.

Albie Richardson-Todd (8)
Loders Primary Academy, Loders

The Evil Marshmallows

I was being chased by an evil marshmallow
Who was bright yellow
He tried to eat my arms and legs off
But instead, I nibbled him
His hair was ice cream
He called in his friends to nibble me
But they were tiny!

Lily Seprenyi-Batten (7)
Loders Primary Academy, Loders

The Big Brick Tunnel

I saw a big brick tunnel
It was as deep and dark as the ocean
Then I entered in carefully
In slow-motion
It was scary
It was slimy as could be
I was scared and confused
But I am glad it was a dream.

Martha Renshaw (8)
Loders Primary Academy, Loders

Minnie Mouse

There it was, the Sealife Centre in all its glory
I decided to enter, enter, enter
I felt happy and excited to see all the fish round me
She was the mouse called Minnie Mouse
And she was my best friend forever.

Mia Andrews (8)
Loders Primary Academy, Loders

Dream Land

I drifted off into a dream
where flying turtles scream
until...
the turtle steals
my banana peel
they run
and plan to have more fun
I was stunned
well, I had fun.

Ella Wiscombe (9)
Loders Primary Academy, Loders

The Evil Marshmallows

I made it to the yummy, sticky marshmallows shop,
As I saw no marshmallows were there!
Tickles on my feet as soft as a mouse,
As I looked down, I screamed louder than a dinosaur.

Elsie Shaw (8)
Loders Primary Academy, Loders

Space

I can see planets in space,
I feel happy,
I was walking on the moon,
Then aliens were coming to get me,
I saw aliens in a flying saucer spin around.

Michael Hughes (7)
Loders Primary Academy, Loders

My School Of Magic

I remember being dropped off at some sort of castle and saw someone with a long hat and old, with long hair. I cried as they adored me. Once I stopped, they held me with their long fingers. They put me in a bed with a blue blanket, put me in and they sang me a song, but weird.
In the morning, it was still dark but they gave me a bowl of sloppy something, but I ate it. Then I fell asleep...
I woke up to be looking big. They said, "Come, let's go." They took me somewhere and I saw other children, they stared at me.
As I stared at them, they said, "There's a new student." The teacher said, "We have a new student. You can sit down over there. Today, we are learning to defeat a dragon."
So we went out and they gave us wands. Then it clicked in my head, I was in a magic school. Then I felt someone tapping me and suddenly, I woke up to find out I was safe at home and it was all a dream.

Manha Khan (10)
Lote Tree Primary School, Foleshill

Above The Sand

I can feel the frothy, foamy, creamy waves
Coming in on my feet,

The crystal-clear water
With silver-scaled fish,
The smiling dolphins and octopuses,
The shining golden shells,
And hidden pearls,
The jewels that cover the soft, sandy floor,

Now, as I go in deeper,
I find something more valuable than
Treasure,
Something I would never see
Above the spray, salty water,
The explosions of a whale,
More satisfying to watch,

Something like a sunken ship,
Covered in mystical creatures and plants,
There are golden stems
And blue roots of every colour,
Now my favourite part,
I tell you my deepest secret,

Be careful not to tell anyone,
Coral reef! Ssh, wait, don't
Tell, please!

Suraiya Limbada (11)
Lote Tree Primary School, Foleshill

Monster Under The Bed

I'm snoring in bed,
No clue what's under the bed,
There's a monster under the bed!
"You're being a baby," Mum said.

A red hand wriggles out from the floor,
I wish I'd jump out and run out the door,
Just even thinking about it, it's making me scared even more,
I hear an ear-piercing roar,

Wide-awake, lying down,
I can hear nothing except the monster's sound,
Something pops out from the floor that is round,
I think it's the head with a big, fat crown.

"Aahh!" I scream in bed,
I turn the lamp and face my fear and look under the bed,
The hand was strangling me under the bed,
I wake up and realise I'm safe and sound in bed.

Aaminah Rashid (11)
Lote Tree Primary School, Foleshill

Battlefield

B attle is so scary when you're in it
A n enemy is not important to me
T o the battlefield, I go
T en people at a time, I kill
L osers hide in the bunkers
E ven the strongest are nervous
F or a dime, I don't care
I report to the barracks
E nd of the battle is relieving
L ots of people are dead
D o you like battles?

Abubakar Hussein (10)
Lote Tree Primary School, Foleshill

Curiosity

The waves call upon the mighty sky
As Marcus discovers a dark, unknown cave
Saddened, Marcus silently starts to cry
Telling his lost mind to behave

Marcus started to worry for his sister
Then, suddenly, a mysterious voice said, "Hello, mister!"
Panicking, Marcus crashes into a wall
While the voice commands him to stand tall

Marcus dashed out of the cave, into the woods
And sees a little cabin, maybe filled with tasty goods
Hungry Marcus' curiosity gets the best of him
While he ran to the cabin, he tripped and lost a limb

Puzzled, Marcus tried to grab his fallen arm
But it started to violently shake, starting from his palm
Suddenly, Marcus' arm started wilting away
Marcus ran toward the arm but was stopped by the smell of chicken filet

Running to the cabin, Marcus thought there was some nice food
Only to realise, was it really that nice and good?

Wondering about the food, his hunger and curiosity started to win
Marcus then started walking into the cabin

Then Marcus found a cosy-looking bed, so he had a little snooze
Though he was hungry and tired, so he had to choose
Between a tasty meal or a comfy bed
He had decided to sleep but then suddenly hurt his head

Turns out, it was a nightmarish transition
Was it all just a dream? Marcus thought
Then he saw his sister next to some delicious food
So his instincts told him, he had a food fight, he fought.

Sayon Irugalbandara (9)
Oldbury Park Primary School, Worcester

Flying Dreams

A dream afar, like outer space
Or trying to tie my shoelace
Playing video games all day long
And suddenly see a monkey who is King Kong

Also, dreams have magic powers
Like making a grape very, very sour
Or making someone into a toad

There is only a bit of time
But will still have a chance to rhyme
Also, you can still taste stuff like limes
Bang! I can hear the saucepans go, *clang!*

I like those dreams, they're wild
They force us to do naughty stuff
There is also a nightmare of someone tough
He is not nice and scares people

Not all are dreams, they could be an aspiration for when you grow
You turn into an engineer and work for Euro tow
Or be a person who will do a quiz
But if I am not famous, I will still remember though.

Frederic Dollochin (9)
Oldbury Park Primary School, Worcester

The Galaxy

Blasting off to space in a huge rocket,
Seeing the flames is so shocking.

Looking at the moon,
We will be there soon!

Travelling through the galaxy,
Feeling ever so happy.

The sun's red flames are so bright,
Little fires in the night.

Mars is red, dreams in your head,
Oh, what a shiny sight,
Saturn's rings are very bright.

Neptune is as blue as can be,
What beautiful sights we can see.

Mercury is like a meteor,
Let's go and see much more.

Jupiter's made of gas,
And this still wasn't the last!

The stars are so bright,
Why do some think it's a fright?

Caitlin Wheal (8)
Oldbury Park Primary School, Worcester

The Nightmare Of Jabba The Hut

Tucked up tightly in your bed,
Jabba the Hut is in your head.

He's creeping, crawling in your thoughts,
Never will you be taught,
The blob is just a scary thought.

Jabba will appear at night and nothing,
No, nothing is in sight,
People running in fright,
A puppy ruffing,
All in fear.

Now that beast is getting near,
There is so much more to fear,
But you reach a cliff,
You fall stiff...

Jabba the Hut is no longer here,
Your freedom is so, so near,
In a tremble, in a shake,
Your thoughts and head are awake.

No more Jabba,
No more fright,
You are now home in delight.

Emily Eden (9)
Oldbury Park Primary School, Worcester

A New Planet In Space

Last night, I had a dream.
It had the most amazing things you have seen.
It was me, making Candyland.
And it was a new brand.
I made a planet that is sweet.
Whoever goes there, thinks it's a treat.
I stood on Earth and stood on the granite.
I jumped to the new planet like a rabbit.
I saw a race and saw the start.
I also saw a red and yellow cart.
I decided to jump to the start.
I noticed a big chart.
I decided I didn't want to.
Because it was difficult to do.
I saw a door made from toffee.
The river I saw was made from coffee.
Then I woke up in the morning.
I saw the sun dawning.

Jacob Shaw (9)
Oldbury Park Primary School, Worcester

Dragon On A Cloud

All through the night
The lanterns shone with no fright
A girl is on a soft cloud
She stood proud
Down, down, she went with no fear
She cried with no tears
She saw a cave
She waved.

In she went, with no tears
Suddenly, she saw her fear
Down, she went, with no fright
She saw a dragon in her sight
The dragon swooped, his wings out
On a mound
The girl cried
The dragon flies.

The girl leapt behind
The dragon's mind cried
The girl ran with fright
The girl grabbed the sword with might
That was the end of the fearless girl.

Josie Stone (9)
Oldbury Park Primary School, Worcester

My Only Dream

My only dream is to play for Aston Villa
So I can play in a claret and blue layer.
I would really, really like
To be the front cover of Nike.

It would be really cool to get the new kit
So I did not get stuck in a pit.
The footballs would be cool but
I could mix it up with a pool.

I could be made up of iron
But I would act like a lion.
I will always be aflame
But I will never get the blame.

It will be a scavenge
But I can take on any challenge.
This is my only dream
But I will be supreme.

Arlo Holding (8)
Oldbury Park Primary School, Worcester

Night Sky

Shooting stars shimmer so
Bright, clear to see
In the night sky
Different shapes and
Sizes and fill the sky
And to see at night
When it's so dark
But so bright as
Little light in the
Big constellations
And the stars are
A lot there, but
The clouds cover
The stars but
They shimmer bright
In the night sky
The stars are big
And small fireballs
All different colours
Way up high
In the sky, stars are
Like memories but in the sky.

Addison Roper (9)
Oldbury Park Primary School, Worcester

The Sand Monster And The Warrior

You're in your perfect dream
But what does it seem?
A monster of sand
Devours a band!

It looks for a weapon
Then out from heaven
Comes a long mace
So you think you've struck ace
But it gobbles you up
Along with a pup!

You try to break loose
But it is no use
So you turn to abuse
You punch a big hole
And crawl out like a mole
You climb the ribcage
And find a dead page
You jump out the face
And look at the place.

Archie Shellam (9)
Oldbury Park Primary School, Worcester

Huzzah Hogwarts

In Hogwarts, there was a great light
That was illuminating the night.
We went into a cavern,
Lit by a single lantern,
We didn't see a phantom.
A feast in the Great Hall
That's as big as a wall,
And not one that's small.
In the common room,
I heard a big boom.
I thought it was a Weasly,
I was right and they looked queasy.
My first lesson was Potions,
I felt lots of emotions.
In Transfiguration,
I turned a cup into a Dalmatian.

Geordie Shellam (9)
Oldbury Park Primary School, Worcester

Trying To Sleep: Dragon Edition

Goodnight,
Sleep tight,
As you dream away,
Dreaming and dreaming,
Sleeping but not screaming.

Dreaming in a way,
Sleeping every day,
Dragons hot like boiling kettles,
They can burn metal.

A colourful castle appeared,
Wondering what just came here,
You enter the castle with fear,
You don't need to stay,
Dragons are flying away.

But it's just a dream,
Goodnight,
Sleep tight.

Cassidy Konzvo (9)
Oldbury Park Primary School, Worcester

The Demon Of The Night

Once, late at night,
I was on a flight,
And everyone had a fright,
There was a demon of the night.

I heard a scary cry,
And saw the demon guy,
And looked up at the midnight sky,
So I didn't see the scary demon guy.

I thought I'd go insane,
But someone called my name,
As I woke up, it was plain
That my nightmare had all been a game.

Bobby Morris (8)
Oldbury Park Primary School, Worcester

The Young Astronaut

So young
So little
But just
Because she's
Little, doesn't
Mean that
Her dreams
Are small

She dreams
Of being
An astronaut
She looks
Up to
The sky
Every night
And says
"One day
I'll be
Up there
In my
Amazing rocket

Across the
Night sky."

Beatrix Richardson (9)
Oldbury Park Primary School, Worcester

Twilight Nights

Tucked up tightly
In your bed
Nightmare thoughts cloud your head
Of forests and bats
You're without a map
Goblins and ghosts
Scare you the most!
Deep, deep down
Looking like a clown
But now I'm awake
Everything is fine
I'm pretty as a shrine.

Ivy Cartwright (9)
Oldbury Park Primary School, Worcester

Football Dream

Tucked up tightly in my bed
Football is the only thing
Running through my head
The only dream I've got
(And I want it quite a lot)
Is being a football player.

Timur Kircu (9)
Oldbury Park Primary School, Worcester

It Was All A Bad Dream

I don't know where I am,
and I haven't got a plan.

I trip with a thud,
and land in some mud.

Then I hear a bang,
followed by a loud clang.

Then I crawl out of the grime
to find myself touching slime.

I hear a manic laugh,
looked above me and gasped.

It was a clown
wearing a crown.

I looked around for some light,
but he looked like he wanted to fight.

Finally, I saw some light,
maybe I could outrun this fight.

I started running,
I felt more cunning.

I fell down a hole,
then grabbed onto a pole.

Still sliding down,
I was starting to drown.

Then it was all over.

I woke up and found out...

It was all a bad dream.

Maggie Gambs (10)
Petworth Primary School, Petworth

Clowns' Island

Jeremy is sailing at night,
In the distance, appears an island in sight,
Nearing the shore,
He spies a house with a big red door,
Standing inside is a clown,
With nothing on his face but a frown,
In his hand was a balloon that popped,
It was then he decided, at this island, he shouldn't have stopped,
Suddenly, more clowns came out,
He couldn't do anything else but shout!
Clowns started to come around,
But Jeremy was forced not to make a sound...

Bethany Kent (10)
Petworth Primary School, Petworth

That's What Makes Me Happy

Marching giraffes munching strawberries
Rainbow dogs dancing to a song
Doing arts and crafts, standing on your head
That's what makes me happy

Family, summer BBQs
Front-flips on a trampoline
Baking sugar cookies with my siblings
That's what makes me happy

Rugby players eating raspberries
Reading books on a netball court
Singing in the rain while sketching a drawing
That's what makes me happy.

Sienna Boddy (9)
Petworth Primary School, Petworth

Lightning Bolt

The lightning lights the lovely night sky,
Why are people afraid? I don't know why,
Lightning doesn't frighten me at all.

Lightning, thunder, I hear it all,
Trains making lightning, carrying coal,
Lightning doesn't frighten me at all.

Striking, stunning, keep on running,
Hurry up, I hear it coming,
Lightning doesn't frighten me at all.

Lyla Anderson (10)
Petworth Primary School, Petworth

Shrek's Swamp

S o where am I? This isn't Book Wonderland, so how about we take a look around?
H ow wonderful is this place? But I need to finish this case
R acks and racks of potions and different motions
E nough talking about stupid potions and let's be aware of the big green monster called Shrek
K icking and snoring, I see, sleeping upon the clouds, he looks so deep
S leeping and sleeping, please, wake up, I want to see your magnificent face

S hiny and old, how luscious are these books? Just like my friend, Ruby-doo, the silly little princess
W ell, where is this book to save my auntie?
A untie, oh Auntie, I found the book, when will you get better? Please, hurry up!
M y auntie, the monster woke up and he's angry
P lease, come and save me before he gets me.

Daisy-Mai Catherine (10)
Springfield Academy, Darlington

The Magical World

One morning, a spook came out the door,
as I stood up and saw paper on the floor.
I picked up the letter. As I read it, I got a fright.
I ran to my dad as my jaw dropped dead.
He read the letter as my heart pumped
blood to my veins.
After an hour's drive, we went to London.
Through the door we went.
As we walked to a shop, I saw a box.
I picked it up.
As I saw a wand in the box,
I picked it up.
A spell, we got.
I paid for one and we were gone.
As I walked onto the train and sat down,
I saw a boy with ginger hair and some freckles.
They stared at me while I stared back.
I saw they hated me. I left with a smirk on my face.
As we were done leaving the train,
we went to the castle.
Everyone was staring at me, as
they saw us get sorted into houses.

As I lay down, I woke up,
I saw myself in my bed.

Paige Hodgson (10)
Springfield Academy, Darlington

A Sky Full Of Stars

Stars glow in the night sky, floating so very high.
I dream of what they look like, jewels sparkling so, so bright,
A sky full of stars, dreaming about going to Mars.
I dreamed about going in a rocket, going so high in the sky.
A sky full of stars.
Years and years went by and it's nearly time to go to space.

The day came by and I had a fright,
The rocket came up and I went inside.
And to space, I went,
The rocket came fast and time was a blast,
I saw a glow in the sky, the stars were here.
I went out of the rocket and floated to a star, shining bright,
My dream came true.
A sky full of stars!

Joshua Tang (10)
Springfield Academy, Darlington

The Dragon

There was a dragon in a cave
And when he saw me, he waved
And when people see him, they scream
As loud as a child in bed
And when he goes outside
People run forever
And never look back for weeks
And when the dragon goes to the village
People assume and loom
And always expect something else
And now they will never change
Now he goes to his cave
And he was sad, mad and glad
He didn't live in the village
And they had weapons for protection and profession
And when dragons blow fire
Humans blow more fire to their admirers
They hope to be the same as the pillagers or villagers.

Theo Aldus (11)
Springfield Academy, Darlington

Trapped

Trapped in a movie,
No one can hear me.
A broken train,
Ignited in a flame.
The spirits chase me,
They clearly hate me.

It's a dream, just a dream.

This is Utopia Station,
Does it belong to a nation?
There's people hiding,
Yet no one crying.
They are quite near,
Soon, they'll be here.

It's a dream, just a dream.

As they approach,
They're faster than a coach.
Eventually, they came,
It ended like a game.

As I awoke,
I thought I was having a stroke.

It was a dream, just a dream.

Brian Lin (11)
Springfield Academy, Darlington

Norman And Me

N othing or anything stops us
O r else you'll have spikes in your back
R oaming through the night with me beside him
M oaning because we're scared with a deadly fright
A nd he's never alone
N obody hurts us hedgehogs, or gets a surprise

A nybody could help, but not around
N obody helps Norman and me
D on't come close, we're very deadly

M eaning is, we're scared
E ven though we've got each other!

Tyler Thompson (10)
Springfield Academy, Darlington

A Space Journey

I wave goodbye,
And shoot up into the sky,

The speed as fast as lightning,
It's a little bit frightening,

I'm right about the Earth, this doesn't feel real,
But it's quite exciting, like my favourite meal,

Floating around and around, due to no gravity,
But I best brush my teeth or I may catch a cavity,

Eating food from packets,
Yet no tennis balls, no rackets,

With no family, no friends,
I close my eyes and the day slowly ends!

Preeya Aujla (11)
Springfield Academy, Darlington

Millie The Dolphin

They come out in the daylight,
They come out at dawn.

They live in sparkling seas,
They never look the same.

They're all around me on my magical island,
They're all special, but one is magical.

They make me feel magic, happy and confused,
They jump up and down like a clown in a box.

They watch it fly in the sky like a butterfly,
They have patterns on their skin,
They became my best friends.

Neave Coglan (11)
Springfield Academy, Darlington

The Castle

This castle is old,
And quite bold.
Nothing in sight,
But bright lights.

It's just a dream,
You'll be thinking.

You'll jump a mile,
Then start to squeal.
This time, this place,
It's a nightmare.

It's just a dream,
You'll be thinking.

You'll be awake,
With a stroke.
You'll have a fright,
In the middle of the night.

Jacob Bullock (10)
Springfield Academy, Darlington

The Island

I woke up on an island,
I felt really shocked,
I got a big fright,
I didn't know what I could eat,
I could only see green coconuts,
I saw palm trees with bananas on them,
I saw the blue, dark ocean,
I noticed something moving,
I looked down and saw a shark,
I wanted to see if there were any more islands,
I needed to find some drinking water.

Romany-Rose Mcmain (11)
Springfield Academy, Darlington

Portals

P aralysis in fear of sight
O f the mysterious creature, it's a fright
R otting trees is such a shame for the freak
T he irregular dreams and horrors are unique
A mazing sight of interesting images of roses red
L azy people that I really dread
S o annoying, but at least I have my friend and something I can cook.

Jessica Wilson (11)
Springfield Academy, Darlington

The Upgrade And Me

U pgrade, upgrade, how nice is this place?
P ictures and posters along the walls
G ood enough? Nah, it has a pit with balls
R ound and round, school goes on
A lso, I love this a ton!
D oughnuts and sweets, wow, this school has taste!
E ven though I wouldn't know my fate.

Charlie Hauxwell (11)
Springfield Academy, Darlington

The Dream I Always Want To Be

I had a dream that I can be as free as I can be
Then I saw a beautiful tree
That was the best climbing space you could go
And there were even sparkling rainbows that I loved
Just to let you know
And now I will tell you about the beautiful sea
Where I go with my besties
All night long, we are making tea
And being funny
Being goofy like a bunny
It was super, super funny
We were so funny
We went and earned a lot of money
I said hello, but I had to go
To make rainbows
For the world to see
I will see you next time
My buzzing bees.

Lennie Clements (9)
St Edmund's Catholic Primary School, Milwall

Phoenix

One day, I had a dream,
there was a phoenix by my side,
I had it guiding me,
it told me to think
about a story in my head.

When I thought of a story,
I told him,
it started off like this,
a girl was rich,
and the phoenix included
that there was another phoenix,
I included the phoenix,
so there was a rich girl,
she loved making fun of
poor people,
she would even
knock out their cups of change,
and the phoenix said
to stop doing this,
but she ignored the phoenix.

She just continued,
just knocking down cups of change,
the girl had a dream that she was poor,
she panicked, she quickly ran
into the streets and begged
for money,
as people knocked her cup down.
She realised how she may be
treating others,
and she never did it again.

Vanessa Plaka (7)
St Edmund's Catholic Primary School, Milwall

Hogwarts Escape

Once upon a time, a baby,
the mum was scary,
but the dad was
a bit of a fizz,
when he grew up,
then he was in the tub,

he realised he had a scar,
but then he opened a bar,
he went to a school
where there was a pool,
and wands,

he had fun,
but lots of buns,
people were talking
about Voldemort walking
in the sky,
but can he fly?

He wanted to attack,
but he got a bat,
he attacked, but saw
him, so he had a law,

get a bat,
but don't call it a fact,

he ate and ran,
he ran to Voldemort with a fan,
he flew away, badly,
people were treated badly,
so he went home.

Milan Jambrich (8)
St Edmund's Catholic Primary School, Milwall

Towers

Zori and her wolf, Dizzie, off they drift,
They find themselves in a dream,
A nightmare, in a tower,
This dream was not as easy as cookies and cream,
Zori ran and ran,
'Til she could no more,
Dizzie hoped
She'd find the exit door,
But not any,
This door was in fact,
Not empty!
Monsters fled out,
Chased them down,
And Dizzie fell
On the wood that was brown,
A trapdoor,
Down, they fell,
And they were stuck
In a hall,
Then they woke up, scared out of their minds,
That dream was one-of-a-kind.

Penny Page (9)
St Edmund's Catholic Primary School, Milwall

Maths World

In my world of numerals,
Big and tiny,
Mathematics made people shiny,
In place value, digits are fun,
But my favourite is number one,

In addition, there is sum and take-away,
With which I can play in the month of May,
Multiplication joined the fun,
Started to run to find the sum,
Division came to join the run,

Finally, fractions
Are friends with division,
On completion, I got permission
To watch some television,
So, little mathematicians, do not worry
On the table of forty.

Porus Sabharwal (7)
St Edmund's Catholic Primary School, Milwall

Famous Athlete Dancer

F or a challenge, you need a leech
A nd the challenge is to teach
M ouse-like crawling around
O ut in the mansion
U may be seeking
S ucked up or bitten

A nd you may be scared
T he reason why is fair
H ow to do it is easy
L et the fun be peasy
E at and
T each all day long
E at, teach

D ay
A nd
N ight
C are all day
E at all day and
R est all day.

Nehvika Arora (7)
St Edmund's Catholic Primary School, Milwall

Lemonade Stand

L emonade, please get one
E at some cookies and have one!
M armalade jam with bread
O n the hot day, wash your head
N o snake here, do not get scared
A nd bread sandwich is layered
D enmark, no lemonade
E lephant, not in here, don't get scared

S ummer came here, get some treats
T ea and coffee in other shops
A nd if you get hurt, we have first aid
N o, we don't have a maid
D o not run away!

Aashvi Mohila (8)
St Edmund's Catholic Primary School, Milwall

Amazing Dream

One amazing night,
I saw a little kite,
With a bunny,
It didn't have any money.

It was in a space,
A pink was the base,
The space was pink,
Little bunny winked.

It was next to the sea,
It was all I could see,
There was another one,
He was eating a bun.

Next to the stars,
There was Mars,
And in there,
Was a bear.

The bear was funny,
Unlike the bunny,
But it was all a dream,
An amazing dream.

Lily Jeon (9)
St Edmund's Catholic Primary School, Milwall

The Dancing Rabbits

In a little dream, there was a bunny,
Hop, hop, tip-top, run, run,
Dance all for fun,
A little rabbit, it said,
"Let's have fun or go on a run!
Want a lollipop or a treat?
I have someone special to meet -
The Queen of Rabbits, she'll tell you a story,
I will be a glory."
"Oh no, you look tired,
You must have had too much,
You must go to bed," he said.
Good night, sweet dreams,
As he dashed away with more beans.

Talita Quintana Fortunato De Carvalho (8)
St Edmund's Catholic Primary School, Milwall

Fabulously Famous

One night, in May, it was almost my birthday
Just one day away and I kicked a tray
My foot was in pain and then I saw a lane
I saw Sabrina Carpenter with an old bartender
And I met a man called Alexander
I made a trend, Sabrina helped me
Ow, I hit a tree and then I found a key
It looked pretty to me
I opened a door to my fans
I said hello to the fans and made them dance
In advance.

Gene Cutler (8)
St Edmund's Catholic Primary School, Milwall

Dance Stage

D early happy behind the stage
A nd because of this, people rage
N ot that nice, but I'm fine
C ircus opens in a line
E verybody cheers, hooray!

S tanding, worried, thinking bad
T aking my pills and becoming rad
A nd taking scissors, snip, snip, snap
G enerated hands, beat, beat, rap
E ven though I'm in a flap.

Antonia Parsons
St Edmund's Catholic Primary School, Milwall

The Dinosaurs

I'm lying down with a frown
I see a dinosaur above my head
While my friend's still in bed
I wake them up, with no luck
They're still in bed with no head
So I don't stay because it was one metre away
It was not a fun day
Then it ate my class, so I threw a glass
It chased me, it was never meant to be
I got them back, we were all a happy family.

Esmé-Rose Murphy (8)
St Edmund's Catholic Primary School, Milwall

The Dancer

Once, there was
a little girl
nine years old
and her fears
were seeing
a real-life
dancer.

And one day
her dreams
came true
and her favourite
dancer, Laughter
Lilly came to
her house.

And she was
very happy
but then she
became flappy, so
she couldn't
move and she
was in shock.

Hazel John-Lewis (8)
St Edmund's Catholic Primary School, Milwall

What Are You Going To Be In The Future?

What can I be?
Shall I be me?
Shall I be cool?
Or shall I be a fool?

Shall I be a builder
Who's secretly a murderer?
But every kill
I pay a bill

I need to use my mind
I can't be mad, I need to find
Let's do this
I can't say bliss

Oh no
I'm in a show
I'm on live
Rated five.

Zakaria Ahmed (9)
St Edmund's Catholic Primary School, Milwall

A Dream

I had a dream and I walked across a beam,
I saw a rainbow, so I hit my toe,
I flew, so I hid, I saw my pet, hi, bye,
I read a book and it gave me good looks,
I learned Spanish and said hola! And I fixed my dog's collar,
I went to a party and my friend, Max, had a big fart,
I went home and watched my phone,
Goodnight, I had a good kite.

Lacey Clements (9)
St Edmund's Catholic Primary School, Milwall

Once Upon A Dream

Once upon a dream
And I never screamed
I hate nightmares
And also dares

I love astronauts
So I always thought
I am a writer
And not a biter

I don't want to be a teacher
And not get bitten by a screecher
I liked an athlete
So I could meet.

Rithvik Jijin (9)
St Edmund's Catholic Primary School, Milwall

The Evil Fairy Who Ruined It All

Once upon a dream,
A fairy gave a scream,
There were once two ladies
Named Lauren and Lara,
Lauren was as
Sweet as honey,
While Lara was as
Energetic as a lightbulb.

They met sixteen fairies,
They all looked the same,
They all talked the same,
And they all walked the same!
Lauren and Lara found it strange,
But they thought it was just a coincidence,
And moved on.

Then all the sixteen fairies disappeared,
And it was the evil fairy
All along...
Then, *boom!*
A girl woke up and realised it was all a dream...

Lara Brogan (8)
Tummery Primary School, Omagh

A Magical Dream

Once upon a dream,
I went to a cafe with ice cream,
A pink fairy eating ice cream,
I got some honey,
And it looked funny.

The fairy and I got some tea,
We drank some tea and the fairy looked at me,
I looked at the old rusty door,
And poured more delicious tea,
I went through the door,
And flew on a sparkling floor.

It brought me to so much more...
I couldn't believe my eyes,
There was a gnome in my eyes,
I didn't want to say goodbye,
I ran back through the door,
I went home and let out a snore.

Maddie Quinn (9)
Tummery Primary School, Omagh

Out Of This World

Once upon a dream,
The world is not as it seems,
Out of this world, what a buzz!
Lots of cats floating with fuzz,
But one little girl, hoping with love,
What could I be?
Just little old me.

I see, I see,
Not little old me,
An astronaut, I can be,
A great big beam grew across my face,
Now I'm going to go to space,

What is this world?
I see a cactus waving at me,
What a delight,
While I'm swooping through the night,
It's not quite right,
I open my eyes, very slight,
Night-night...

Tierna O'Neill (8)
Tummery Primary School, Omagh

Alone

I wake up in a sack,
All is black,
I can't get back,
I must have been kidnapped,
With trust, I charge
The sack,

Out I come, but
There is a man in black,
He has the broken sack,
He draws his gun as if it is fun,
So I run, run, run!
He gives chase, but he can't
Keep up the pace,

Now I am safe,
Who was my kidnapper?
I hear creepy laughing,
I hear a rustle beyond the trees, oh no!
I'm all alone,
Just then, I wake up,
Safe at home,
That was the worst dream.

Nico Simpson (9)
Tummery Primary School, Omagh

A Wonderful Day

I woke up, I noticed something new,
I looked up and saw something blue,
I heard a noise,
It was talking toys,
Then I looked around and saw some pies,
Then I looked up to the skies,

A pie appeared with legs and arms,
Would it do any harm?
Talking toys appeared in front of me,
I didn't know how to be,

So I ran, scared and afraid,
Then I tripped and hurt my leg,
I saw a panda,
He put out his hand to get me home,
To rest in my bed with a gnome,
Then I gently drifted off and fell asleep.

Quinn McDermott (8)
Tummery Primary School, Omagh

The Fairies

Once I woke up, it was strange,
A new range,
My room, so much smoke,
Out of the blue,
Something new,
No smoke, but glitter instead.

A glittering fairy appeared,
In front of me,
It flutters away,
I follow it,
It led me out of my house,
I look at my house,

A gingerbread house, it was the fairy,
It changed my world,
About six more appeared,
Dolls grew on trees,
Unicorns, dragons,
What an amazing world,
I woke up in my bed, what a dream!

Hannah McCormac (8)
Tummery Primary School, Omagh

A Candy Swirl

Once upon a dream,
I was in a candy swirl,
Eating a Twirl,
A fairy appeared, called Pearl,

Poisonous potions everywhere,
In her eyes, she had a glare,
She had a sparkle in her hair,
It made the people stop and stare,

A magic, sparkly spider appeared,
I thought most spiders looked weird,
With bright beards,
They left me in tears,

Then she got back home,
On a magic comb,
Her sofa was as high as a throne,
She fell asleep as she let out a moan.

Ellie Sheridan (8)
Tummery Primary School, Omagh

The Magical Forest

Into the forest, off we go,
Leaving terrific trails as we flow,
With a magical crow,
Who is very slow.

I saw a tiny mist,
So I decided to make a list
Of all the things I missed,
And I sent it to my sis'.

With dancing feet,
Not on the street,
The ponies had their treats,
Before they all fell asleep.

I said goodnight,
As the morning grew light,
All the creatures were out of sight,
I love them with all my might.

Dara O'Neill (8)
Tummery Primary School, Omagh

The Fluffy Cat

Last night, I had a dream
That I have a cat called Queen
She loves to sleep on her mat
And at night, she chases rats

She loves to snuggle on the mat
With her favourite toy, called Pat
She also likes to sleep on my lap
And loves to clap

But the cat left my lap
And did a clap
She sat on the mat
With her toy, called Pat

But then I slipped on the mat
And gave her a big fright
And the cat jumped on to my fluffy hat!

Rosie Barrett (9)
Tummery Primary School, Omagh

Flying Horses

Once upon a dream,
Horses are my favourite theme,
They always make me beam,

My favourite horse is Tilly,
With her little filly,
They love to be silly,
I called Tilly's filly, Billy,

As I turned around,
To see it could not be true,
Do loop-de-loops through the air,
It was like being at a fair!
Then... *poof!*

I woke up and realised it was all just a dream,
Or was it?

Karen Gibson (8)
Tummery Primary School, Omagh

I Become A YouTuber

I had a dream last night
It gave me quite a fright
I became a YouTuber overnight
It made me full of delight

I love to watch lots of videos
And give my opinion on a ratio
I speak a lot
And play a lot of video games on the trot

I upload video games on the internet
To make my viewers interact
I made lots of money in what I do
And I do it all for you.

Dara Doherty (8)
Tummery Primary School, Omagh

Nightmare

N othing could help me in this world
I could not wake up last night
G ames were going on in my brain
H ere I was, in a mountain
T here were zombies everywhere
M y hands were freezing to ice
A nd
R apid zombies were around me
E xhausted, I was about to freeze, but then I woke up.

Luke Brogan (9)
Tummery Primary School, Omagh

The Forest Dream To A Beach

Once upon a dream
I had this dream
about me, something
gleaming, going to me
people mowing the
lawns.

Mother and daughter bonds together
together forever
loved.

Branches falling
branches falling to
trolls, falling
from the sky
singing songs
time flies.

Lauren Golden (8)
Tummery Primary School, Omagh

The Best Dream Ever

I had a dream last night
It gave me a startling fright
I was so excited, I would almost burst
With fear or joy, it was the worst

I love to explore the world around me
From grief to joy
It was fun
But now I have to say goodbye.

Christopher Mimnagh (8)
Tummery Primary School, Omagh

Cheese Moon

We are in outer space
With an alien race
Space is like a lake
That winds like a snake

Lots of room on the moon
To zoom like a rocket, *boom!*
On the moon, there are silly tunes
I can see an alien dance like a baboon

Around and around, my rocket goes
It gets louder and louder like a rumbling volcano
I see an alien with one eye
Oh! Is it a spy?

And one has become my friend
I really don't want this dream to end
I don't have to be scared of this alien thing
Because it's just named me king.

Oscar Baines (9)
Whitegate End Primary & Nursery School, Oldham

Clown And Spiders

There was a clown
In the town
With a smile made of nightmares.
He has a crown made of stolen treasure.
Frightening children gives him pleasure.

He's in my room.
What's he going to do with a broom?
He looks about 100 years old.
He should be in a tomb.

There's a spider
With a glider
Who was making a web to trap a fly
He's in the corner of the room
What a little hider!
When I looked up, there they were
Above my head
This filled me with dread.

Lucas Yao (8)
Whitegate End Primary & Nursery School, Oldham

The Ultimate Sport

Sleeping in the dark,
But you wake up to the sound of a bark.
You're on a basketball pitch with guys trying to beat you.
They boo, but you don't have a clue.
After winning the game, a portal opens,
But as you run through with crying pride,
The portal goes shut!
You landed on a football pitch and the ground shook!
Man of the Match was the prize you took.

Harry Beaumont (8)
Whitegate End Primary & Nursery School, Oldham

The School Nightmare

Oh no, I have to run!
This really isn't fun
Mrs Ejaz is chasing me
As fast as a bumblebee

It's midnight
She's giving me a fright
It's so cruel
I'm going to have a duel

I was in the hall
When I tripped over a ball
But Mrs Ejaz got me
And she put me in the chokey
I hate school
This really isn't cool.

Emily Shenton (9)
Whitegate End Primary & Nursery School, Oldham

Nuke The Nightmare

Last night, I was on Earth
The rocket really hurt
I was eating trash
When I heard a big crash
It was very loud
So there was a massive crowd.

Billy Whaley (9)
Whitegate End Primary & Nursery School, Oldham

The Sea Unicorn Life

There was a human who lived by the sea. She went down on the rocky path to the beach, where the waves crashed on the beach ahead. When she finally got down, there was nothing to hear, which made her shiver in fear.

Suddenly, the silence was broken by a splash in the sea. It made her panic, made her bury herself in the sand so she would be fine. But if she'd have looked, she'd have seen a marvellous sight of rainbows and sparkles above a sea unicorn.

The unicorn found her. She opened a sliver of eye and said, "Phew! You're not a beast or a horrible foe!" The unicorn spoke to the little girl. "You just want to take me to the river below." She said, "Do it tomorrow, I must go!" which made the unicorn whinny with joy.

Oliver Thomas (9)
Yeoford Community Primary School, Yeoford

Dreamz

D isaster strikes! Suddenly, I'm in an endless hallway with a terrifying figure chasing me
R acing, turning, jumping past doors, hoping to find a way back home
E ager to outrun this beast, its long furry hands try to grab me
A mazed at how fast I can run, I see an opened door filled with colours and not a pale brown
M oments later, I pounce through the door but then hear a buzz from an alarm clock
Z ooming fast, but then I realise I'm safe in my bed and away from that thing!

Amelia Abbott (11)
Yeoford Community Primary School, Yeoford

Bouncing High

I lie in bed, late at night
The greatest dreams fill my head
Bouncing high in the sky on a trampoline
Flips and somersaults, the fun never ends
I like to have a good laugh with my friends
One day, I hope to be in the Olympics, maybe very soon
But when I look up at the moon
I suddenly hear a magical tune
Then I realise it was just the most wonderful dream
And I am the happiest I have ever been!

Ellie Clarke (8)
Yeoford Community Primary School, Yeoford

YOUNG WRITERS INFORMATION

We hope you have enjoyed reading this book – and that you will continue to in the coming years.

If you're a young writer who enjoys reading and creative writing, or the parent of an enthusiastic poet or story writer, do visit our website **www.youngwriters.co.uk**. Here you will find free competitions, workshops and games, as well as recommended reads, a poetry glossary and our blog.

If you would like to order further copies of this book, or any of our other titles, then please give us a call or visit **www.youngwriters.co.uk**.

Young Writers
Remus House
Coltsfoot Drive
Peterborough
PE2 9BF
(01733) 890066
info@youngwriters.co.uk

YoungWritersUK **YoungWritersCW**
youngwriterscw **youngwriterscw**